Little Red Riding Hood

Retold by Thea Feldman
Illustrated by J. Ellen Dolce

A GOLDEN BOOK • NEW YORK
Western Publishing Company, Inc., Racine, Wisconsin 53404

Once upon a time a little girl lived with her mother and father in a cozy little cottage at the edge of a deep green forest.

The little girl's grandmother lived at the other end of the forest, and she loved her granddaughter very much. She made her a bright red hooded cloak, which the little girl wore everywhere she went. Everyone knew her as Little Red Riding Hood.

One day Little Red Riding Hood's mother said to her, "I want you to take some food to your grandmother. She has not been feeling well."

She handed Little Red Riding Hood a basket filled with freshly baked carrot cake, fat juicy apples, and fragrant leaves for making tea.

As Little Red Riding Hood set out on her trip,
her mother warned her to stay on the path in the
forest. "Be very careful," she said. "Do not stop
along the way, and do not speak to any strangers."

Little Red Riding Hood was very proud to be given such an important task. She looked straight ahead as she entered the woods and thought of all the merry stories she would tell her grandmother to cheer her.

The tall trees in the forest blocked the sun, casting shadows everywhere. But Little Red Riding Hood could hear the happy songs of the birds, and far off she heard the sounds of woodcutters at work.

Suddenly a huge shadow loomed in front of her. Perched atop a great boulder by the side of the lane was a burly silver-colored wolf with blazing eyes. Little Red Riding Hood gasped in surprise.

   The wolf smiled at Little Red Riding Hood, and
his eyes softened into a kindly gaze. "Where are
you off to, Little Red?" he asked in a deep friendly
voice.

"Why, I'm going to see my grandmother, who
lives at the end of the woods," she said, pointing
in the direction of her grandmother's cottage.
"She's not feeling well, so I'm taking her some
food."

"I'm sure your grandmother will be happy to see you," said the wolf. "Do you know that right around this bend is a beautiful patch of wildflowers? I bet your grandmother would like a nice bouquet of them."

Little Red Riding Hood remembered then that
she was not supposed to stop along the way or
speak to strangers, so she bade the wolf good-bye
and set out again. But when she came upon the
wildflowers, she saw that they were indeed
beautiful, and she stopped to pick just a few.

As for the wolf, he hurried through the woods until he arrived at Grandmother's house. He knocked on the door and said in his highest voice, "Oh, Grandmother, it's Little Red Riding Hood. I've come to see you."

"Come in, dear child," called the old woman.

The wolf s-l-o-w-l-y opened the door, but then—
quick as a wink!—he leapt to the bed and gobbled
up Little Red Riding Hood's grandmother!

He dressed himself in one of Grandmother's
nightgowns and one of her nightcaps and settled
down in her bed to wait for Little Red Riding Hood.

When Little Red Riding Hood got to the cottage
and knocked on the door, a voice inside called
out, "Come right in, my dear." And so the little
girl went in.

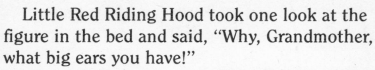

Little Red Riding Hood took one look at the figure in the bed and said, "Why, Grandmother, what big ears you have!"

"The better to hear you with," was the reply.

Little Red Riding Hood moved a bit closer to the bed. "Why, Grandmother, what big eyes you have!"

"The better to see you with."

Little Red Riding Hood moved closer still.

"Oh, Grandmother, what big teeth you have!"
"The better to eat you with," snarled the wolf,
and before Little Red Riding Hood could cry out,
he pounced on her and swallowed her whole!

Now the wolf was very tired, so he dropped off to sleep.

A woodcutter who was in the habit of stopping by every day came to the cottage at the usual time. Amazed to find a sleeping wolf in Grandmother's bed, he quickly guessed what had happened.

At that moment the wolf opened his eyes and ran for his life. But the woodcutter caught him, and with one blow of his axe he killed the wolf and slit open his belly. Out came Little Red Riding Hood and her grandmother!

Then Little Red Riding Hood, her grandmother, and the woodcutter all went back inside the cottage. Little Red Riding Hood made tea, and the woodcutter sliced them all thick pieces of carrot cake. They enjoyed their little feast without giving another thought to the wicked wolf.

And from that day forward, they all lived happily ever after.